The Prince and the Potty

NICHOLAS ALLAN

RED FOX

Some other books by Nicholas Allan:

Cinderella's Bum
Father Christmas Comes Up Trumps!
Father Christmas Needs a Wee!
The Giant's Loo Roll
Jesus' Christmas Party
Jesus' Day Off
Picasso's Trousers
The Royal Nappy
The Queen's Knickers
Where Willy Went

THE PRINCE AND THE POTTY
A RED FOX BOOK 978 1 782 95257 2

Published in Great Britain by Red Fox,
an imprint of Random House Children's Publishers UK
A Random House Group Company

This edition published 2014

1 3 5 7 9 10 8 6 4 2

Red Fox Books are published by Random House Children's Publishers UK,
61–63 Uxbridge Road, London W5 5SA

www.randomhousechildrens.co.uk
www.randomhouse.co.uk

Addresses for companies within The Random House Group Limited can be found at: www.randomhouse.co.uk/offices.htm

THE RANDOM HOUSE GROUP Limited Reg. No. 954009

A CIP catalogue record for this book is available from the British Library.

Printed in China

The Random House Group Limited supports The Forest Stewardship Council® (FSC®), the leading
international forest-certification organisation. Our books carrying the FSC label are printed on FSC®-certified paper.
FSC is the only forest-certification scheme supported by the leading environmental organisations, including Greenpeace.
Our paper procurement policy can be found at www.randomhouse.co.uk/environment

MIX
Paper from
responsible sources
FSC® C104723
FSC
www.fsc.org

The Baby Royal is growing up . . .

. . . so it's time to visit the Royal Potty Workshops.

Royal Potties have been made here since Royalty began.

There is even a Royal Potty Museum with potties
from around the globe.

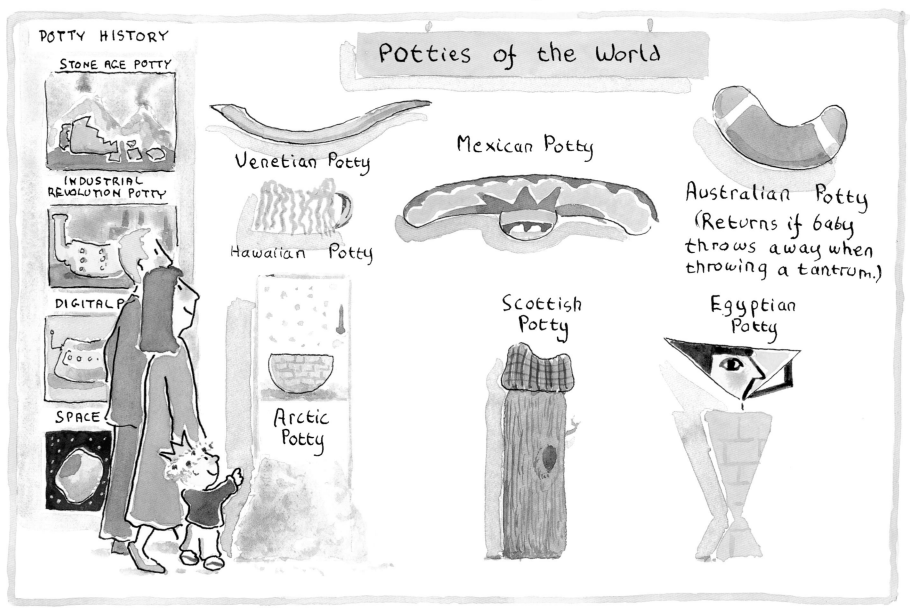

Kings and Queens must learn to use their potties quickly because they cannot rule the country wearing nappies.

Henry VI was only nine months old when he became King! He got his crown and potty at the same time . . .

. . . which must have been a little confusing.

Richard the Lion-Heart liked fighting a lot.

His potty was very good as a shield . . .

. . . but then not so good as a potty.

"My kingdom for a horse!" cried Richard III when he needed a ride . . .

"My kingdom for a potty!" he must have cried when he needed a wee!

And Elizabeth II was brought up to be Queen
as soon as she was born . . .

So she always used her potty in a most queenly manner.

The Duke and Duchess decide they need a
VIP (Very Important Potty) for their VIP (Very Important Prince).

The Royal Potty Engineer has been hard at work.

But the National Anthem Potty is **TOO LOUD!**

And the Eco-friendly Potty is **TOO ECO-FRIENDLY!**

And the Carriage Potty is not . . . quite . . . fast . . . enough!

Luckily there is one left . . .

HOW ROYAL ROBO-POTTY WORKS

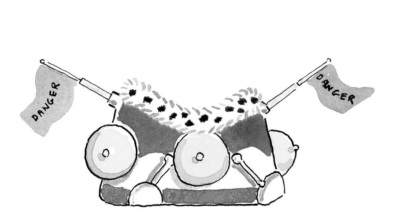

Robo-Potty
has alarm bells
and pop-up
warning flags.

Robo-Potty is
carried in the
Royal Potty Box.

Smelly detector
alarm sounds
when potty
is needed.

But then, one day, the Baby Royal
visits a nursery . . .

. . . and SUDDENLY the Baby Royal
knows ALL BY HIMSELF

that he needs his potty!

BUT WHERE IS IT?

WHERE IS THE ROYAL POTTY?

Oh dear . . .

Looks like Nanny has a problem with her hat.

"Perhaps the Baby Royal would like a nursery potty,"
says the nursery teacher.

"An ordinary potty?" says the Royal Bodyguard.
"Not the Royal Potty?"

"AN ORDINARY POTTY!"
says the Royal Reporter.

"An ORDINARY potty!"
says the Royal Photographer.

"AN ORDINARY POTTY!"
says the Royal Policeman.

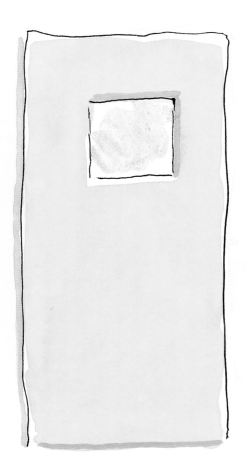

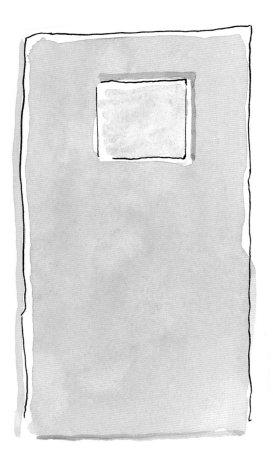

So the Baby Royal goes to find a potty

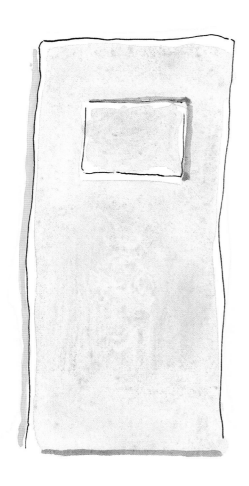

ALL BY HIMSELF!

And he runs and he runs . . .

until, ALL BY HIMSELF . . .

. . . he finds one.

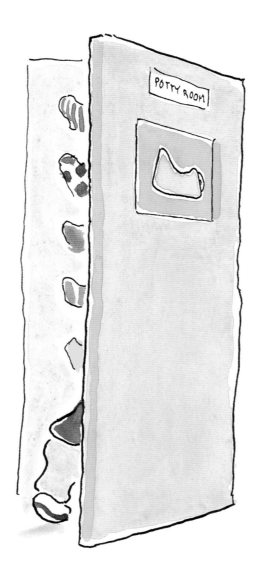

And even though it is an ORDINARY POTTY,
not the Royal Potty . . .

it suits him just fine!

Which just goes to show what a wise King he will become.